The short, repeated phrases on each page make it easy for children to join in the reading. They begin to do this by remembering the story, but gradually learn to match the words they are saying to those they see.

The strong rhythm of this book helps children to almost chant the story. This helps them to remember it and say it aloud to themselves and to you.

Children enjoy talking about books during the reading and afterwards. They might have questions to ask or comments to make. The story may remind them of other familiar books – or train rides!

A ticket collector Smiling at me, That's ...

what I see, That's what I see.

Into the tunnel, All scary and dark – What will I see? What will I see?

We went on a train to Tom's house – not a steam train.

And we nearly missed it.

We hope you enjoy reading this book together.

For Michael Philip
J.C.

For Amelia
S.L.

First published 1995
by Walker Books Ltd
87 Vauxhall Walk
London SE11 5HJ

This edition published 1998

10 9 8 7 6 5 4 3 2 1

Text © 1995 June Crebbin
Illustrations © 1995 Stephen Lambert
Introductory and concluding notes © 1998 CLPE

Printed in Great Britain

ISBN 0-7445-4897-7

Reading Together

The Train Ride

Read it together

The Train Ride is a colourful, rhythmic picture book which tells the story of a child's journey through the countryside to visit his grandmother.

Reading aloud is the best way to help your child get to know and enjoy a book. This book is especially good to read aloud because the pattern of the words makes it sound like a train chugging along!

We're off on a journey Out of the town – What shall I see? What shall I see?

What do you think this story will be about?

A train ride!

Talking together about the story, rhyme and pictures helps children to make sense of the book and increases the pleasure in reading.

The Train Ride

Written by **June Crebbin**   Illustrated by **Stephen Lambert**

WALKER BOOKS
AND SUBSIDIARIES
LONDON · BOSTON · SYDNEY

We're off on a journey

Out of the town –

What shall I see?   What shall I see?

Sheep running off
And cows lying down,

That's what I see,
That's what I see.

Over the meadow,
Up on the hill,

What shall I see?
What shall I see?

A mare and her foal
Standing perfectly still,

That's what I see,
That's what I see.

There is a farm
Down a bumpety road –

What shall I see?
What shall I see?

A shiny red tractor
Pulling its load,

That's what I see,
That's what I see.

Here in my seat,
My lunch on my knee,

What shall I see?
What shall I see?

A ticket collector
Smiling at me,

That's what I see,
That's what I see.

Into the tunnel,
Scary and black –

What shall I see?
What shall I see?

My face in a mirror,
Staring back,

That's what I see,
That's what I see.

After the tunnel –
When we come out –

What shall I see?
What shall I see?

A gaggle of geese
Strutting about,

That's what I see,
That's what I see.

Over the treetops,
High in the sky,

What shall I see?
What shall I see?

A giant balloon
Sailing by,

That's what I see,
That's what I see.

Listen! The engine
Is slowing down –

What shall I see?
What shall I see?

A market square,
A seaside town,

That's what I see,
That's what I see.

There is the lighthouse,   The sand and the sea…

Here is the station –

Who shall I see?

There is my grandma

Welcoming me…

Welcoming

me.

Read it again

**Welcoming me...
Wel ... com ... ing
... me.**

Tap out the rhythm

The story is written to sound like the rhythm
of a train going along. You could tap out the
rhythm of the train ride as you read it together,
slowing down as it reaches the end of the journey.

Taking part

The strong repetition makes it easy for children to join in
with the story. After reading it several times, leave gaps for your child
to say the sections in green: *"That's what I see, That's what I see."*

Naming game

You can spend time looking at the pictures together,
naming all the different things that can be seen from the
train window. Some of them are good for counting, too.

**There's a
red tractor
and two
sheep.**

Map the journey

Use this map to describe the journey to visit grandma in the story.
Where did they start and what did they see along the way? You can
look back at the book to help you.

STATION

houses

sheep

cows

farm and tractor

cornfield

mare and foal

I Spy

Journeys can seem shorter and more enjoyable if wordgames are played along the way. You can play alphabet games on any family journeys you take, or just walking to the playgroup or the shops.

I spy with my little eye something beginning with "c".

Cow? Cloud? Cup!

Ticket collectors

Children often like to make collections. They could involve the family in collecting tickets of all kinds to keep in a scrapbook, with labels explaining each one:

Mum takes a bus to work.
We went on a train to the seaside.
Grandpa took me to the zoo.
(Postcards could be included, too.)

balloon

STATION

viaduct

nnel

geese

Reading Together

The *Reading Together* series is divided into four levels – starting with red, then on to yellow, blue and finally green. The six books in each level offer children varied experiences of reading. There are stories, poems, rhymes and songs, traditional tales and information books to choose from.

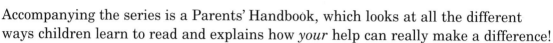

Accompanying the series is a Parents' Handbook, which looks at all the different ways children learn to read and explains how *your* help can really make a difference!